SHATNER QUAKE

SHATNER QUAKE

JEFF BURK

Eraserhead Press
Portland, OR

This is a work of parody, as defined by the Fair Use Doctrine. Any similarities, without satirical intent, to copyrighted characters, or individuals living or dead, are purely coincidental.

ERASERHEAD PRESS
205 NE BRYANT
PORTLAND, OR 97211

WWW.ERASERHEADPRESS.COM

ISBN: 1-933929-82-0

Dear William Shatner,

This work is a tribute to you. Not an attempt to mock, ridicule, or belittle you.

You are the quintessential postmodern man. You have made a career out of playing a caricature of yourself. Your entire life has become an elaborate work of performance art. Who can tell when you are acting and when you are just being crazy Shatner? I know I can't.

There is no line between fantasy and reality when it comes to your work. For that I salute you.

Real life is so boring. But while the rest of us attempt to find some escape from our normal world of drudgery, you take a different approach. You remake the world in your own image. You're an accomplished actor, writer, singer, and all around crazy-cool person. I bet when you walk down the street people and vehicles part before you in honor of your Shatnertastic self.

This is your world, the rest of us just live in it.

So this book is for you, Mr. Shatner, a true renaissance man.

Love,
Jeff Burk

P.S. Please don't sue me.

Shatnerquake is dedicated to the following people:

Angie Molinar, Rose O'Keefe, Carlton Mellick III, Whitney Streed, Jeremy Robert Johnson, Cameron Pierce, and—of course—George Takei

"How do I stay so healthy and boyishly handsome? It's simple. I drink the blood of young runaways."

- William Shatner

CHAPTER ONE

Sniveling little sycophantic shits, thought William Shatner looking from the limo's back seat.

The limo pulled past the front entrance of the hotel and headed for the back.

Thank God, I don't have to deal with them. Yet.

A crowd of several hundred people milled about the colossal arched doorway. Some were dressed in Starfleet uniforms, some dressed as police officers, some in lawyerish suits. Most were simply dressed in jeans and t-shirts. Many of the shirts had Shatner's face plastered on the front.

Shatner looked at the people and he stared back from dozens of different chests.

They were mostly young men but a few women peppered the crowd.

At least I might get some tail out of this.

Shatner arched his neck to get a better look at the hotel. The Cathode-La was the largest, most advanced convention center in the world, featuring four full-sized theaters, a cafeteria and six restaurants, twenty-three bars, more large empty rooms than one could even count, and enough lodging to hold a medium-sized army.

The building was a squat, white cube the size of one-hundred city blocks. A mostly ugly piece of architecture, except for the front entrance. A large glass pane, at least a hundred feet wide, sat in the concrete. It almost reached the roof but the top of the glass came to a rounded point before it got there. Its shape felt more appropriate in a church behind the altar than on a multi-billion dollar corporate structure.

At the glass' base were dozens of revolving doors leading into the Cathode-La's main lobby. The doors were flanked by two massive white columns that stood as high as the building. In between them hung a huge white banner. "Welcome to ShatnerCon!" was printed on it in black scripted letters.

As the limo pulled around the corner of the building a lone man sitting on the ground caught Shatner's eye. He wore a t-shirt with Bruce Campbell in the *Army of Darkness* movie-poster pose on the front. He held a cardboard sign with the crude, hand-written message: "Alright you Primitive Screwheads, listen up! Don't follow the False Messiah!"

The man raised his right arm and waved a stump wrapped in white fabric at the passing limo. Shatner felt a shiver go down his spine even though he was sure the limo's tinted windows prevented the man from seeing inside.

Fucking Campbellians. They're even here.

William Shatner had no personal problem with Bruce Campbell. He understood that Bruce was just another actor trying to squeak out a living in the dog-eat-dog world of entertainment. Shatner just wished that he would stop encouraging his followers to destroy all those who competed for the straight-to-video dollars. The constant death threats and assassination attempts were getting annoying.

The limo went down the side of the building. Things were much less active over here.

The parking lot stretched away from the building as

far as one could see and every space was filled. Throughout the maze of vehicles, scattered people were heading in the direction of the front entrance.

After a few minutes the limo rounded another corner of the building and pulled to a smooth stop.

Here we go. Put on that pretty public face.

Shatner got out of the limo and found himself standing at a maintenance door with a woman in her late thirties next to it. She was dressed in a black skirt, a black suit jacket with black shirt underneath, and black pumps. She was holding a clipboard with one hand and a half-smoked cigarette with the other.

"Mr. Shatner," she said nodding. She brought the cigarette to her mouth and breathed in deeply. The rest of the cigarette was immediately reduced to long gray ash. She breathed out a cloud.

"That's...me," Shatner said smiling broadly and trying not to cough.

The woman tossed the butt away and extended her hand.

"I'm Natalie Albright, we've spoken on the phone. You're eight minutes late," she said as they shook hands.

"Follow me please." She turned around and opened the maintenance door.

Shatner sneaked a look at her ass as he followed her in.

They were in a white hallway with a lush purple carpet floor. Natalie walked quickly down the hall and Shatner hurried to keep up.

"Over the next four days we have you scheduled for fifteen events. I recommend that you start preparing your acceptance speech for the 'Achievements in Exceptional Shatnerisms' Award Banquet now. You will be expected to speak for at least three hours."

The two rounded a corner and were going down another identical hallway.

"How…are you doing? Things… going smoothly so far?" asked Shatner. *Come on, turn on that Shatner-charm.*

"Everything's functioning smoothly outside of your late arrival." Natalie checked her watch.

"So are…we headed…to my room?" asked Shatner. It was obvious he wasn't going to get anywhere with her. She was all business.

"Oh, no."

They turned another corner and were standing in front of a door.

"Your first signing was supposed to start four minutes ago."

Natalie pushed open the door. On the other side was a plain steel table. Sitting on each side of the table were three foot high stacks of Polaroid press-shots. In the center of the table was a single silver magic-marker.

Two large men dressed in riot gear stood on the other side of the table. They were facing the huge line of people that extended all the way across the several-hundred feet long room and out the door on the other side.

Shatner stepped out into the room and it exploded in cheers as the crowd saw their hero.

Give them what they want.

Shatner flashed a huge grin and waved his arms at the delirious acolytes.

"How long," he said, turning back to Natalie, "am I here for?"

"An autograph was included in the price of admission. This is your first block for tickets numbered A01 to AAA54. It shouldn't take you more than eight hours."

Eight-fucking-hours! At least they're paying me a fortune for this.

Shatner did his best to maintain his cheerful smile as he moved behind the table. He picked up the marker and popped the cap off as the two guards moved aside.

The first fan stepped forward and Shatner almost gasped aloud in horror. The man looked identical to Shatner— from his face to his hair to his body build and height.

"It is an honor to finally meet you." The man even had the same voice.

It took all of his skills as a public entertainer for Shatner to not give away his shock.

The fan placed a copy of *TekWar* on the table and put out his hand. "I'm Bob Chaplin."

Shatner turned back on and shook his hand. "Wow… it's…just… like looking into a mirror." He gestured at their clothes, "We're…even wearing the same suits." They were each dressed in navy blue suits, white undershirt, and pale blue ties with slanted white stripes.

The fan blushed. "It was really quite easy to figure out which outfit you would go with. You wear roughly the same thirteen configurations for public appearances. There was then the consideration of major con versus minor con, this obviously being a major con. That eliminated six possibilities. From there it was a simple matter of reviewing your last twenty-eight appearances and comparing that to your public dress history."

Behind him Shatner heard a static-distorted voice, "Ms. Albright, we have a 2517."

Shatner looked behind him and saw Natalie stepping away from the table and raising a walkie-talkie to her mouth.

"Could you sign it to: My Number 1 Fan, Bob?"

15

Shatner turned his attention back to the fan. He opened the book and started to write on the title page.

He could hear Natalie's hushed voice quickly talking. She sounded pissed.

"That's…a little creepy…like *Misery*," Shatner said chucking and handing the book back to Bob.

"What?"

"You know…Kathy Bates…the Stephen King movie."

Bob stared blankly. "I don't think I do."

Natalie was suddenly standing next to Shatner and placed a hand on his shoulder. "Bill, we got a problem in the theaters that I need to go take care of. I'll be back in just a few minutes."

Oh my God, she's going to leave me alone with these people.

"Now don't worry about anything, we have plenty of security," she motioned to the guards who had moved to either side of the table. They stood tall and stoic, facing forward. They looked like police officers, but their black uniforms bore no insignia. Their heads were covered with black helmets with black face-shields pulled down.

Shatner did not feel any more at ease.

"Someone will be along shortly with water and can take an order for anything else you may want."

Before he had a chance to respond, Natalie was through the door.

Bob beamed an adoring smile. "The cosmetic surgery cost a fortune. The voice-box reshaping alone was sixty thousand dollars."

Shatner beamed a smile right back. "Money well spent."

CHAPTER TWO

The convention's theater was a marvel of modern movie-going. Four screens, each ten stories high. Three stories of seating gave each theater a capacity of around two thousand. Even though it was early in the first day of the convention, the theaters were already three-quarters of the way full.

Rick was alone in the projection booth, sitting on the floor and smoking a joint. He listened to the footage being played. William Shatner was cursing as he blew a contestant's prize money on The *$20,000 Pyramid*. It made him proud that they were able to get a hold of the unedited footage.

For the convention, the Cathode-La was holding a four day, twenty-four hours a day William Shatner marathon. Each of the fours screens was continuously playing movies, shows, and other footage from Shatner's career.

Rick was in charge of the projector for the day shifts in Theater Three. It was an easy gig, once every hour or so he had to change the film reel. Outside of that, there was not really anything else to do. The booth also provided a good smoke-spot in the crowded hotel.

I hope I get to meet him, thought Rick as he took another hit, *but I bet he's a dick in real life.*

He coughed out the smoke as a voice came over

his walkie-talkie. "Anyone else seeing a light behind their screen?" It was Michael from theater one.

Rick stood up and looked out of the booth. On the screen Shatner was throwing a chair and storming off the set. At the bottom center a glowing blue light was distorting the image. It looked as if someone had turned on a blue lamp behind the movie screen.

"I got it too," said Rick into the walkie-talkie. Two more voices came over. Emily and Jacob from Theaters Two and Four also were seeing it.

"Rick, go check it out," ordered Michael.

Rick sighed. "OK."

He took another drag from the joint and snuffed it out as he left the projection booth.

* * *

Natalie shut the door behind herself as she entered the room. She carefully and calmly bolted the door and pulled out a cigarette. She lit it and regarded the figure in the center.

A man sat hunched over in a wooden chair. He wore black jeans and a black *Maniac Cop* t-shirt. He was missing his right hand, the sure sign of a Campbellian.

The man lifted his head and both his eyes were blue bruised shut. His bottom lip was split open and clotted blood coated his chin.

Directly above the man hung a bare light bulb. The light brightly illuminated the center of the room but left the edges bathed in black.

On the left and right side of the man stood convention guards in the darkness.

"We found him in the backstage halls of the theater,"

said the guard on the right.

"He won't talk yet," said the guard on the left.

Natalie took two long steps forward and stood directly in front of the man. She sucked in almost the entire cigarette, leaving only a stub of burning ember.

"He will," she said through plumes of smoke.

She grabbed his right arm and put out the butt on the scarred stump.

* * *

"While on the set of TJ Hooker, which make and model of car did you find the most comfortable to hang off of?"

Shatner signed a DVD set of the *Original Series* and handed it back to a pimply teen wearing a home made cardboard communicator on a red sweater. The teen giggled and scurried off, clutching his new prized possession.

"I never really... took notice," said Shatner as he took a nine-by-twelve photo from the next person in line, curiously wearing a *Battlestar Galatica* shirt. Bob glared at him until his picture was signed and he walked away.

Bob watched him until he was halfway across the room and then asked, "Was it emotionally hard on *Rescue 911* being constantly surrounded, I mean mentally, by so much trauma?"

Shatner smiled at the next person in line. At least Bob had enough sense to stand by the side of the table and let others pass by.

"I'm a... professional," said Shatner, "I can deal... with anything."

Stay professional. Stay professional. Stay professional. Stay...

JEFF BURK

* * *

Rick stepped into the back screen room. It wasn't really a room; each of the walls were the backside of each of the theater's four screens. Rick could see four backwards Shatners, completely surrounding him.

The theaters were soundproofed from each other but in the back screen room there was no soundproofing. The noise from all four showings blended together. Lounge-crooning merged with electronic beeping and police sirens with a laugh-track accompaniment.

In the center of the bare floor was a VCR. The side panels were removed and wires jutted out from its mechanical viscera. On top of the machine were two blue light bulbs.

Rick stepped closer to the VCR and then took notice of the front display screen. *55...54...53...52...*

Rick held up his walkie-talkie, "I got something back here..."

* * *

Natalie walked over to a table against the back wall of the room. She picked up a rag and wiped the blood off her hands.

She walked back to the Campellian and lit up another cigarette. He lay on the floor in a fetal position. The chair he was sitting on now lay shattered against the left wall.

He rolled and softly cried, cradling his left arm. It now ended in a bloody stump. Strips of flesh hung from the crude wound.

He tried to get to his feet but he was woozy from blood loss. He tried to use his stumps for more support.

20

The combination of pain and the blood-slicked floor were too much for his weakened state. The stumps slipped out from beneath him and he crashed down.

Natalie snickered.

"Fiction Bomb," he weakly said.

"What!" Natalie crouched down and grabbed his hair. She pulled his head back and screamed, "What the fuck did you just say?"

"There's a Fiction Bomb behind the theaters' screens."

Natalie stood up and kicked the man in the face.

Fiction Bombs were the result of the Network Wars. They were devices that, when set off near film stock, erase the media from reality. No one remembers the entertainment. There are no records of the entertainment. It completely disappears. They were illegal, but certain terrorist sects and unscrupulous networks were still known to use them.

Natalie rushed to the room's door. She turned back and addressed the convention guards, "Sodomize him with his hand until he tells you how many other Campbellians are here. If he doesn't talk in two minutes, kill him."

* * *

Shatner signed and signed while Bob talked and talked.

* * *

"It's a Fiction Bomb!" yelled Michael over the walkie-talkie.

"What?" said Rick.

"I just got off with Natalie," replied Michael, "It's a

21

Fiction Bomb! Turn it off!"

Rick dropped the walkie-talkie and rushed toward the Fiction Bomb. He grabbed it and began tearing wires from the side. He picked up the device and smashed it against the floor. Both light bulbs shattered into glass shards that pierced his hands in a dozen places.

Rick picked up the black box with bleeding fingers and looked at the display.

2...1...

If the blast had not immediately liquefied Rick and splattered him onto the screens in a billion droplets, he could have taken comfort in the fact that he had fucked up the Fiction Bomb enough so it did not work properly.

Those in the theaters heard a loud blast and saw the screens become red-tinted as Rick hit them. Then the blast hit them, reducing all those in the theaters and projection booths to piles of gray ash.

The theaters and the screens, however, remained unharmed. The films showing flickered and then the images disappeared. They glowed a bright, vivid dark blue and moved erratically in and out—as if alive and struggling to take a breath. In the blue, shapes began to move. They took form and grew limbs and heads.

These blue figures danced around the screens and then began to smoothly step out of the picture. They began to move about the now-empty theaters and become more defined figures.

One figure formed a brown suit and a briefcase.

One twirled its microphone about by the cord.

One flipped open his communicator. "Captain to ship. Captain to ship." No one answered.

More and more figures emerged from the screens.

At first they were without feeling but, as they became

whole, this new world filled their senses.

First came the feeling that they didn't belong—some fundamental urge that this world was not for them. That they were pale shadows of something else already here.

Then the anger.

Then the desire to do something about it.

CHAPTER THREE

Dealer's Room: The room quaked and shook when the Fiction Bomb went off. An unnatural hush swept over the crowd as everyone waited to see what would happen next.

A voice came over the room's PA system: "We have just received notice that a generator blew out on one of the lower levels. We apologize for the inconvenience but there is nothing to worry about. Thank you."

Larry and Jay stood in the center of the room listening to the announcement.

"Do you think anything's wrong?" asked Jay.

"Nah, they just said it was a generator blowing out," replied Larry who had already lost interest in the blast as he noticed the rare *Star Trek: Dinosaur Planet* with matching seven inch record on a nearby table.

Most of the crowd was absorbed again in the merchandise for sale. A few still milled about, unsure of what to do and if the announcement was completely truthful.

From where Jay stood he could see through the doorways of the dealer's room and into one of the convention's hallways. At that moment a young couple ran past his view—the woman sobbing and the man's eyes blank with shock.

SHATNERQUAKE

"I don't know," said Jay, "I've got a bad feeling."

"Man, chill. Check it out. Naked pics of Nichelle Nichols."

"Ooooooooooo!"

Lobby: Emma held her breath as the display cases shook. Leading to the registration table were several massive displays of Shatner memorabilia to entertain attendees waiting in the seemingly endless registration line. When the blast happened, they all shook and Emma had mental images of millions of dollars in collectables being destroyed and Natalie blaming her for the accident.

Fortunately, the cases were quickly steadied and crisis was averted.

Emma breathed out a sigh of relief and she leaned back into what she thought was the wall. Instead, she leaned against a twelve foot high display of all the various weapons that William Shatner had used in one-on-one to the death battles as Captain Kirk. It was a massive wooden display with the weapons mounted for the attendees viewing pleasure. The props had been kept in pristine condition over the years and many were still deadly sharp.

Her weight unbalanced the large display and it started to sway. Emma spun around and tried steadying it, but she was not strong enough and her actions only worsened the rocking. The lirpa that Kirk used against Spock in "Amok Time" fell and missed her head by inches.

That was close-

All the weapons came spilling down and she was pierced in a dozen places by a variety of daggers, swords, and pole arms. None of the wounds were deadly, so she was still alive. However, the many weapons had gone through her body and straight into the floor, trapping her in place. All she could do was moan through the pain paralysis. The

25

convention attendees were too concerned with losing their place in line to come help her.

A camera flashed as someone took a picture.

The case rocked back and forth once more and then tipped over, mashing her into the carpet.

Emma Lombardi was the first, but far from last, fatality at ShatnerCon.

Signing Room: Shatner stood up, "What the…fuck… was that?"

A wave of panic passed through those in the room. The crowd's orderly line began to dissolve and people began to move en mass to the signing table.

The two guards moved in front of the table and produced batons. They held them out and ready.

"Sir, please go through the door and move on to another area," barked one of the guards. Neither made any movement so it was unclear which one actually spoke.

"I just," Shatner waved his arms, "got here. I don't know…where…anything is."

The guards didn't respond. There was now a solid wall of people on the other side of the table, calling out to Shatner for an autograph or asking the guards what the blast was.

"Where's…the green room?" asked Shatner.

"Sir, you need to leave," ordered the guard, his voice harsher this time.

Bob was still off to the side, "I'll come with you Mr. Shatner."

He motioned to move forward and the guard closest to him pivoted and shoved him hard with the baton. Bob stumbled back and fell over into the crowd, taking two people down with him.

Shatner flinched. He didn't like the guy, but it is strange watching yourself get hurt.

He went through the door and was back in the hallway. On this side of the door he could not hear any of the pandemonium from the signing room. He looked up and down the hallways but he couldn't remember which direction he had come from.

He pulled out his cell phone and scrolled through the contacts and found Natalie's number. He hit dial and put the phone to his ear. Nothing happened. He looked at the display, it said "Calling" but he did not hear any ringing. He hung up and tried again, this time waiting while the display read "Calling." Still nothing.

Shit.

With only two choices, he picked left and started walking. After rounding a corner he came to a door that opened to a stairwell. It only went up and since he really did not have a better option he went up. At the first landing, he came to a door and went through it.

He stood in a giant open room filled with glass displays. Shatner walked to the case next to the fire exit he had just come through. It was filled with small microphones, the kind you clip onto a shirt lapel. Each one had a place card with a show name and date on it. It took a moment before the significance occured to him. The cards were all shows that he was a guest on and the date was when he was there. The microphones were the very mics he wore on the shows.

He turned around and looked at the other cases. They held costumes, props, toys, and other memorabilia. Shatner was in a museum dedicated to himself.

There were six other people in the area Shatner was in and they were all now staring at him. Shatner quickly moved to the far end of the room where there was a doorway leading into the museum's next exhibit.

There was also a magazine rack holding a display of convention programs, their fronts were a full-cover image of Shatner with his charming smile.

Shatner grabbed one of the programs. He held it up to his face to block peoples' views as he quickly moved deeper into the museum.

CHAPTER FOUR

Captain Kirk walked with a confident stride. The hall was filled with people worried about the blast they had just heard and felt. Most paid Kirk little mind, a few complimented him on his costume.

Kirk eyed the people and wondered what kind of world he was on where people wore such outlandish outfits.

He spied, at the end of the hall, someone in a red Starfleet uniform. Kirk sprinted down the hall, dodging around the convention goers.

"Thank...God," Kirk said placing his hand on the man's shoulder, "I...thought...I...was the only one stranded here."

The portly man stood a foot taller than Kirk. He sneered at Kirk.

"What's...the...situation," asked Kirk.

"You mean the noise? I don't know man. The people running the con say a generator in the basement overloaded. You mind taking your hand..."

"Hold...on," Kirk interrupted. He pulled out his phaser and pointed across the hall, "a Klingon!"

The man looked and there was someone standing in a costume modeled after the Klingons on the *Original Series.*

The "Klingon" saw them looking and arched a large eyebrow. He laughed and jokingly raised his plastic disrupter.

"Watch out," yelled Kirk as he raised and fired his phaser. The Klingon screamed in anguish as his body disintegrated.

People all around began screaming and running to get away from the madman with a laser gun.

"Come." Kirk again grabbed the Starfleet officer's shoulder, "let's…move on."

Kirk started running down the hallway and the man followed, afraid of what would happen if he did not.

In the panic that phasering Jordan Mitchells, Klingon enthusiast, caused, Lorene Devonport was trampled by no less than seven overweight science fiction lovers. As she lay dying, broken bones piercing her lungs, she saw the image of William Shatner hovering above her. He looked down and smiled at her. She smiled back.

He turned around and faced no one in particular. "There is a limit to the abuse the human body can sustain. Hello, I'm William Shatner. Tonight, on a special convention edition of *Rescue 911*, we observe the case of Lorene Devonport, left battered and broken. Will anyone arrive to help her in time?"

How does William Shatner know my name? was Lorene's last thought.

"We would like to remind you," he continued, "all the footage in this segment is real."

* * *

Shatner walked from room to room in the museum, unable to find the way out of this maze of his past. Each room was at least one hundred feet by one hundred feet with huge doorways at either end. As he walked on, Shatner could find no hint of an exit.

As he went further into the maze the displays got stranger. At first they were mostly obsessive props and tickets from his various shows and movies. Now he was coming across displays labeled WILLIAM SHATNER'S BABY TEETH and WILLIAM SHATNER'S KIDNEY STONES. The weirdest was the glass case purported to be a display of used condoms for which he was responsible. He was not sure how the convention organizers had gotten a hold of them and thought it better not to consider the implications for too long.

Worse, he was now getting a crowd following him. The program was not providing enough of a disguise. There were now around twenty curious fans following him through the maze. If he didn't find a way out soon the crowd was sure to grow. He hurried on hoping to find an exit or someone in charge.

He went through the doorway into the next room and saw at the far end another person who had a crowd following him. The person got closer and Shatner could see through the glass display cases the blue uniform of a police officer.

Shatner ran around the cases and up to the officer, "Oh thank God, I..." He froze in midsentence as he stared into the face of TJ Hooker.

It's just one of those damn impersonators.

Shatner turned to walk away when Hooker punched him in the side of the head. Shatner stumbled back and fell through a display case, sending broken glass and used q-tips flying. He sat in the shattered glass and held his head, a thin line of blood trickling down from his temple.

"What...the hell's...the matter with you?"

Hooker grabbed Shatner by his collar. "I'm taking you down scum." He lifted Shatner to his feet and threw him into the wall. Shatner fell to the ground but was quickly back to his feet, his Drunken Shaolin Street Fighting skills kicking in.

After being swarmed and nearly crushed to a gooey pulp by overzealous fans at the One Weekend on Earth Convention in '96, Shatner dedicated two hours of his day, every day, to the ancient Chinese art. It came in handy at times like these when an autograph seeker did not know his place.

Hooker came running forward. Shatner grabbed him by his arms and used his force to throw him headfirst into one of the display cases. Hooker crashed through and lay on the ground stunned.

One of the first lessons one is taught in the martial arts is that the best way not to lose a fight is to not get into one. With this in mind, Shatner took off running, a crowd of screaming, cheering fans following him.

* * *

"Mother-fuck, shit shit shit," said Natalie as she stomped her feet. She breathed in deeply and exhaled, attempting to calm herself down.

She raised the walkie-talkie, "So you lost William Shatner."

There was a pause and a static filtered voice said, "Yes, ma'am."

"Well fucking find him," Natalie yelled and then hung the walkie-talkie on its belt holster.

She took out her cell phone and dialed Shatner's

number. The screen read: CALL FAILED. She tried two more times with the same result.

"Son-of-a-bitch!" She put the phone back in her pocket. Just one more problem she did not need.

She began to walk in the direction of the main entrance. If Shatner was wandering around, there was a good chance he would head there hoping to find convention staff. This was the abso-fucking-lutely worst time for him to go missing. The guards had learned from the prisoner that there were three other Campbellians loose in the convention. Unfortunately, the prisoner did not reveal where they were or what their plans were before he finally died from massive blood loss.

The halls were fairly empty as most of the convention goers were attending events. But there were still people milling about talking and trading trivia. There was a slight tension in the air from the blast but the convention staff was telling everyone that it was just a generator blowing out. The story seemed to sit well with the attendees. No one wanted to believe that anything actually was wrong. That would mean an end to the whole fun filled weekend that everyone had paid good money to attend.

Someone grabbed Natalie's shoulder. She spun around and looked into the face of William Shatner.

"Oh, thank G—" The words stalled in her throat when she got a good look at him. His clothes were faded gray and his skin was a sickly chalk color.

"Vi…aspekti simlia…iu…en pargi," he said in poorly spoken Esperanto. Translation: You…look like… someone…in charge.

"What the hell?" said Natalie. This was not Shatner. He looked way too young and thin. But he was the spitting image of an early Shatner.

33

"Kio…estas loko…kie mi?" Translation: What…is this place…where am I?

Natalie backed away, turned and hurried down the hall.

She looked over her shoulder and saw the Shatner look-alike babbling to some other attendee.

Goddamn, things are getting weird.

* * *

Bruce, Bruce, and Bruce peered out from behind the massive cardboard cut-out of Jaba the Hutt.

"What the hell is he doing?" asked Bruce.

The three Campbellians were watching what appeared to be William Shatner doing an impromptu concert for a small crowd of fans. Right now, he was in the middle of his immortal rendition of "Lucy in the Sky with Diamonds."

"I think he's singing," said Bruce.

"You'd think he'd want everyone to forget about that aspect of his career," said Bruce as she sat down. The large cardboard Hutt blocked any chance of Shatner seeing her.

"He's just looking for attention," said Bruce as he sat down next to her.

"OK, remember what we're here for," said Bruce bringing the team back to their mission. "We wait until he finishes this number and then when the crowd is clapping and he's taking his bows, we make our move."

"Right," said Bruce and Bruce in unison.

The three conspirators waited for Shatner to finish.

"I can't believe they got Bruce," said Bruce.

"I don't even want to think about what they're doing to him," said Bruce. Bruce nodded grimly in agreement.

They sat silent while Shatner sang/spoke the last

verse. As he began the chorus for the final time the three Bruces got to their feet. They raised their right, handless arms and bowed their heads in silent prayer to the Almighty Bruce.

As they walked out from behind the intergalactic crime lord cut-out, Shatner finished his song and the gathered crowd applauded.

Bruce slipped his hand into his pants pocket and slid on the set of brass knuckles. He walked briskly up to Shatner, who was too busy taking bows to notice the oncoming threat. Bruce and Bruce moved to his side to provide back-up and, if necessary, crowd control.

Bruce did one last glance around to make sure there were none of those freaky convention guards and then he moved in for the attack.

One quick blow with the brass knuckles knocked Shatner out cold before he had any chance to react. The people in the crowd cried out as they saw their hero crumble to the ground. A brave fan made a move to help but the one-two attack of Bruce and Bruce, each of whom had their own sets of brass knuckles, quickly reduced him to a bleeding quivering heap.

"Anyone else feeling like a hero?" yelled Bruce as she fiercely eyed the crowd. No one was.

Bruce smiled at Bruce. She looked so hot when her blood-lust got pumping.

He rushed over to help Bruce with Shatner's unconscious body. The two began to drag the TV star down the hall while Bruce made sure no one followed them. While she may have been under half the size of most of the convention attendees, she was crazier and fiercer than any of them.

The Bruces rounded a corner to a hallway and dragged

the body through a maintenance door that led to the boiler room. Bruce shortly followed them through the door.

"Did anyone follow?"

"Nah," she said, "they were all too scared."

She walked over to Shatner. "Wow, we actually got him."

The three Bruces stood around the unconscious entertainment icon. They looked down in amazement. They actually managed to get the Great Satan himself.

"OK," said Bruce, "start unpacking the boxes. Let's not waste our opportunity here.

"I admire your determination but I do believe that you've made a mistake."

The Campbellians jumped and spun around. Standing in the doorway was another William Shatner.

"Who the hell are you?" said Bruce.

"I'm Denny Crane," said the Shatner, "the greatest lawyer in the world."

CHAPTER FIVE

Shatner made it through two more rooms of the museum and then paused to catch his breath by a scale replica of his office from *Boston Legal*. People stood in a half-circle around him yelling and clapping.

"What...is wrong...with...you people," Shatner screamed at them.

"aaaaaarrrrgggGGGGHHHHHH!!!!" The crowd parted and Hooker came charging. Shatner grabbed an umbrella from the set and stepped aside, swinging it at Hooker's legs. He went face-first into the ground. The crowd was joyous.

Hooker stood up and faced Shatner. His forehead was cut wide open and thick-black ooze leaked from the wound.

"We can be at this all day," said Hooker, "but, I am taking you down."

Shatner turned and ran into the next room with Hooker hot on his tail. Directly in front of Shatner was the ambulance that he was carried off in from *The Twilight Zone*. He went to dodge around it but Hooker tackled his legs from behind. Shatner fell forward and his head THUNCKED off the vehicle.

The world faded in and out from color to black. Through the haze, Shatner could see Hooker standing over him. Hooker pulled out his police baton and raised it over his head. Shatner's senses shot back and he kicked out his leg, hitting Hooker squarely in the balls. He grabbed his crotch and keeled over.

The crowd laughed and applauded.

Shatner got to his feet. Next to the ambulance there was a small glass display containing the vehicle's key. Shatner covered his hand with his jacket sleeve and punched through the case. He grabbed out the key and held it in his fist; it jutted out from between his index and middle fingers.

He turned and Hooker was already charging, baton held high. Shatner stepped forward and slashed with the key. Black goop splattered on the ambulance and Hooker held his face screaming.

Shatner ran past him to the ambulance, pulled open the driver's side door, and got in. He used the key and turned it on. It roared to life, its engine growling and sounding more like a hotrod than an emergency vehicle from the nineteen fifties.

Shatner revved the engine and shifted the gears out of park. Hooker then threw himself across the hood of the car. Where his right eye was once, now there was a ruined socket of black sludge. He yelled and coughed up black goop onto the windshield. Shatner screamed and hit the gas.

The car shot forward. Hooker held on, coughing and splattering more thick black stuff onto the glass.

Shatner could see well enough to guide the ambulance through the museum's doorways. The vehicle plowed through displays, destroying artifacts of Shatner's public and personal life. Shatner put on his seatbelt, held on tight, and watched his life flash by.

38

SHATNERQUAKE

* * *

Kirk and the man in the Starfleet uniform jogged down the hallway. The man's name was Stephen, not that Kirk had asked, and he was very out of shape. He wheezed and his lungs burned as he tried to keep pace with Kirk. He very desperately wanted to get away but, after seeing what the phaser could do, he did not dare try to escape.

"Please," Stephen said, grasping his chest, "I need a minute."

"OK," Kirk said as he scowled disapprovingly.

Stephen fell against the wall and gasped for breath. Kirk paced about in the hall. They were now far enough away from the scene of the murder that no one was concerned about their presence. The convention attendees walked around Kirk and Stephen.

"Marvelous," said Kirk in amazement as he surveyed the people. A few feet from them was a woman dressed as an Orion slave girl. Her skin was completely painted green and revealing green fabric draped her body. She was talking to a man dressed as a Vulcan.

"Marvelous," Kirk said again, eyeing the woman. Stephen would swear he saw Kirk's eyes sparkle.

Kirk confidently strolled over to her. He stepped in front of the man and leaned against the wall, bracing himself with his elbow.

"You're...wasting...your time." Kirk motioned with his head to the man. "He has...no heart...no feelings...not... like me."

He moved in close to the woman.

"Hey buddy, back the fuck off," said the man. He stood a good foot taller than Kirk.

"What the hell's your problem," said the woman as

39

she began to back away from Kirk. Before she made it far, Kirk grabbed her. He wrapped one arm around her waist, the other around her neck, and pulled her close.

"We shouldn't….fight…there are more…enjoyable… activities for men and women," said Kirk as he leaned his face in.

"Fuck off freak," yelled the woman and she struggled to get out of his vice-like grip.

The man grabbed Kirk and pulled him off the woman with ease. He spun Kirk around and punched him squarely in the jaw. Kirk crumpled to the ground, dazed, as the man and the woman walked off holding hands.

Stephen rushed over. He could not help but feel bad. He had been there more than once.

He crouched down next to Kirk.

"Vulcans…normally…aren't so emotional," said Kirk as Stephen helped him to his feet.

"And…the woman," Kirk massaged his jaw, "they… normally…like me more."

"Come on," said Stephen, "Let's run down some halls. It'll make you feel better."

* * *

Natalie walked into the main lobby and froze when she saw the massive arched glass entrance and what was on the other side of it. She stood still and after a moment lit a cigarette, totally disregarding the convention's no smoking in public places policy. She walked forward and placed her hand on the glass, staring out in disbelief and terror.

The sound of a roaring engine shook her out of her trance. She turned around and looked back at the lobby.

It was a massive room, empty of but a few convention registration tables and a few display cases. She noticed that there was no one working the tables—there was no one else in the room.

The engine became louder. It was coming from ahead of her. On the opposite side of the room was a set of stairs and an escalator that led up to the second floor and the convention's museum.

She then heard screaming and people suddenly came spilling into view, running and tumbling down the stairs and escalator. Then the vehicle came speeding into sight. When it hit the stairs, and people trying to get down them, it was ramped into the air.

Natalie watched in amazement as the vehicle flew through the room. It soared up and down in a graceful arch. *Is that an ambulance* and *why is a man hanging off the hood* were her last two thoughts as it smashed her into the front doors.

CHAPTER SIX

Bob walked up to the film schedule to see what was currently showing. As he read, he absentmindedly rubbed his chest, it was still sore from when the security guard had pushed him. According to the paper, theater two, which he was currently outside of, was in the middle of a *Star Trek* marathon. Bob grinned—this would make him feel better after all the shit that had already happened to him.

The theater had a snack stand window just next to the door. Bob walked up to it and studied the menu. A bag of popcorn was priced at eighteen dollars. Bob gasped. This was an atrocity! But crunchy popcorn coated with greasy movie theater pseudo-butter would surely hit the spot right now.

He stood at the window grumbling to himself over having to endure yet another indignity. His outrage turned to annoyance as no salesperson appeared. He waited a few more minutes and then decided to just go in the theater. He would rather sit and enjoy the adventures of the USS Enterprise than wait for some volunteer who flaked off.

When he entered the theater he was surprised to find it completely empty except for one lone person sitting in the center of the front row. It was strange to see such a large room so barren. Bob walked in and found himself a seat near the center.

The man in front was loudly laughing and clapping his hands. He was oddly amused for an episode of *Star Trek*. Bob tried to ignore him and focus on the show.

It seemed to be an episode that Bob did not immediately recognize, which was strange as he had seen every episode of the *Original Series* sixty-seven times. Spock, McCoy, Sulu, and Chekov were discussing the sudden disappearance of Captain Kirk. The characters seemed more scared and worried than Bob had ever remembered seeing them.

The man in front hooted and Bob took his eyes off the screen to glare at him, but the man was no longer there. Bob sat up to get a better look at the front row. The man really was gone.

Bob sat back, relieved to be rid of the nuisance. He jumped when he realized there was now someone sitting next to him. The man was facing him, with a broad, slightly unhinged smile.

The man leaned closer and Bob gasped when he saw the face of William Shatner.

"Hi, I'm Bill," said the man offering his hand, "my my, you're a good looking fellow."

"Thanks," said Bob shaking his hand, "and we've already met."

"Oh, we have?" the Shatner's left eye twitched, "my mistake."

Then the man was gone. One moment he was sitting next to Bob and the next, the seat was empty. Bob looked around confused and a little unnerved. Perhaps his mother was right and he really was going crazy over William Shatner.

"If you're looking for a good price on airplane tickets,

I know a place."

Bob jumped and spun around, the Shatner was now sitting on his other side.

"…no…thanks." Bob was getting a little scared. He was sure this was not the real William Shatner. His suit was different from what he was wearing earlier and it was not one of his public appearance suits. He was wearing one of the suits that Shatner reserved for commercials.

The man was acting very differently from how Shatner had when Bob met him in the signing room. Bob was also fairly sure the real William Shatner did not have teleporting abilities no matter how bad-ass that would be.

"How about a four star hotel at a two star rate?" eagerly asked the Shatner.

"No, I don't want anything." Bob stood and went to leave. This guy was starting to get to him.

Suddenly the man was in the row behind Bob and placed both of his hands firmly on Bob's shoulders and pushed him back into the seat.

"You're just stressed out. Sit back, relax, enjoy the show, and then we can discuss business," said the Shatner as he started to give Bob a shoulder massage.

Bob would have protested but the Shatner's hands felt so good.

He watched the screen and a Redshirt walked onto the bridge.

"Lieutenant Leslie," said Spock, "what are you doing away from your post?"

Lieutenant Leslie pulled out a phaser and pointed it at Spock. "I'm here because I'm tired of taking orders from you boy scouts. There are going to be some changes around here."

The Shatner continued to knead and his grip was

starting to get a bit uncomfortably hard. Watching the show was not helping Bob. He could feel a primal kind of panic creeping into his head.

There was something very wrong here.

To confirm Bob's suspicions, Lieutenant Leslie phasered Spock on the screen. McCoy ran to hold his dead friend. Leslie stood atop the Captain's chair and let loose a series of laughs that would make a mad scientist proud. Sulu and Chekov bowed in worship of their new master. A chill went down Bob's spine.

He jumped to his feet.

"What's wrong?" asked the Shatner. He sounded genuinely concerned.

"We'll talk business later," shouted Bob as he ran for the exit.

"Come back! I can get you anything you want," called the Shatner as Bob fled from the theater.

* * *

"This is too fucking weird," said Bruce as she paced back and forth. The small meeting room was crowded with people and they were beginning to get to her.

"Calm down," said Bruce. He stood up and walked over to Bruce. He held her shoulders, "I know, I know. But think of it. We're going to be heroes, saints for the Bruce on high."

She hugged Bruce, tears streaming down her face. "I know, but this is all a little much to handle."

"This is very touching," Bruce and Bruce turned to face Denny Crane, "but time is wasting."

Crane held out his hand, "so do we have a partnership?"

45

Bruce let go of Bruce and shook Crane's hand.

"Excellent," said Crane, "once you do what you need to…he's ours."

The room was then full of excitement and talking. Bruce wiped the tears from her face and looked at the roomful of Shatners. Through her blurred vision she could not tell any of them apart.

She looked to Bruce who was standing next to Denny Crane. Crane's smile was too big for her taste. She then looked to Bruce who was leaning against the side wall and had been remaining awfully quiet. His eyes met hers and he nodded at her.

"Too fucking weird," he said.

* * *

Natalie could hear a strange buzzing sound but see only black. From somewhere nearby came the scent of strawberries. She felt very cold.

The buzzing turned into a low drone as her vision faded in.

She found herself looking through the windshield of the old ambulance at a banged and bloodied Shatner.

About fucking time I found him.

She tried to move but could not. Her body felt strange, her waist throbbed and she could not feel her legs. She looked down and screamed.

Her body had been cut completely in half by the vehicle. Her torso was sitting upright on the hood of the ambulance and that was all that was holding in her innards. Thick, dark blood oozed from where she met the metal.

"Despite suffering extreme physical trauma, Natalie

Albright remained conscious and aware of her situation."

Natalie stifled her cries and looked to see another Shatner standing next to the wreckage. He was standing near the wreckage but was not looking at her. He was staring intently off into the corner of the room. She looked in that direction but there was nothing there.

"Please. Help me," she said.

"Victims of similar injuries have been known to live hours after having the incapacitating incident. But they never survive movement attempts by rescuers."

"Please."

"Will she survive or will she be yet another tragic story on this already dreadful day. Stay tuned to this special convention edition of Rescue 911."

He stood still and stared straight ahead, waiting for the commercials to start. Natalie weakly coughed up black speckled blood.

"And we're off," said the Shatner as his pose noticeably relaxed. He reached into his pants pocket and took out a handful of chocolate candies. He popped one into his mouth.

"This is gonna be really great stuff," he said through a full mouth. "Full of drama. You're really good. Oh, here, you want one?"

The Shatner tossed her a piece of candy and Natalie reached to catch it purely out of reflex. The sudden movement was enough to throw off her balance and she tipped over. Her torso hit the metal with a dull thump. She moaned low as her blood and insides rushed out.

The Shatner chewed and watched the red wave of viscera rush down the hood of the ambulance. Natalie tried lifting an arm toward him but it fell down limp.

He regarded the situation for a moment and then

went walking off in search of the next segment.

* * *

Shatner coughed and woke up still strapped into the ambulance seat. He unbuckled his seatbelt, opened the door, and fell out of the smoking, mangled vehicle. He crawled forward a few feet on his hands and knees, coughing.

He got to his feet and was amazed to find himself uninjured. His suit was torn in a few places, but other than that he was unscathed. He turned to the wreckage and saw that he was the only one who made it out OK.

Natalie had been severed in half at the waist by the air-born ambulance. The top half of her was on the roof. A splatter-trail of entrails led from the front of the vehicle to the lower half of her body, which was next to the debris.

TJ Hooker had been crushed between the ambulance and the doors, his chest cavity torn wide open. Spilling out from the huge wound were bucketfuls of the black goop and what looked to be film stock. The reels looked like they had been tightly stuffed in his body but were now unwound out onto the vehicle's hood.

Shatner was less concerned about this strange sight then he was over the entrance. It looked like someone had placed a giant television on the other side, the channel turned to dead static. Every inch of the glass was displaying the snow show. He stood staring at the strange sight and then moved to one of the front doors the flying ambulance did not destroy.

He pushed at the revolving door but it would not budge.

He rushed back to the center of the lobby. By now

other people had wandered into the room and had noticed the wall of static on the other side of the exit. They were so distracted by the sight that they did not even notice that THE William Shatner was amongst them.

Shatner ran over to the registration table and grabbed a map of the convention. He looked it over, trying to figure out what to do next. The convention staff had been no help so far and what the fuck was with TJ Hooker trying to kill him?

He studied the various room listings. Theater? No. Filking? No. Fan Fiction Readings? No. Dealer's Room?

That was it. The Dealer's Room was most likely where the other guests for the convention would be. Shatner flipped through the program, trying to find the guest list but could not.

No matter. The Dealer's Room is just down that hall. There will be someone there that can help me. Someone like me. A celebrity.

Shatner went jogging in the direction of the Dealer's Room as the lobby filled with shocked and worried convention attendees.

CHAPTER SEVEN

Kirk and Stephen jogged through the doorway. Kirk froze and dropped to his knees.

"What kind...of fantastic...bazaar...is this?" asked Kirk surveying the huge table-filled room.

Stephen leaned wheezing against the wall. "It's just the Dealer's Room."

"You're in...terrible shape...for a...Starfleet officer," said Kirk as he took out his tricorder and tried yet again to get a reading. He shook his head. "Still nothing."

Kirk clapped his hand on Steven's shoulder, "Come on, Redshirt... let's explore...this...feast for the senses... You don't mind if I call you Redshirt...do you?"

* * *

Shatner walked into the Dealer's room amazed at its size and scope, just like everything else he had seen at the convention so far. The room was at least as large as three football fields. The entire floor-space was taken up with tables of dealers selling their wares and convention attendees eager to empty their wallets. The panic and chaos that was happening elsewhere in the convention did not seem to have reached here yet.

Shatner pushed his way into the crowd, hoping to find a celebrity's table or a convention worker that could direct him to where he could find one. He squeezed his way past fat collectors arguing over the printing number of action figures and dealers attempting to overcharge for limited edition Christmas tree ornaments. It was so busy and crowded that no one took notice of him.

After going down the third row of tables he was beginning to lose hope that he could find anyone to help him.

"Bill! Thank God I found you."

Shatner spun around at the sound of his own voice, ready to fight. He looked into the mirror version of himself and relaxed. It was just Bob.

Bob looked very concerned. "There is some really strange shit going down around here. There are versions of you running around all over the place."

"What...do...you mean?" Shatner said, thinking about his encounter with the TJ Hooker look alike.

"I'm not one-hundred percent sure, but I have a theory," said Bob. Shatner groaned and rolled his eyes. Bob ignored him and continued, "Remember the Network Wars of a few years back? Remember the fiction bombs? Celebrated Teletician, Jonah Epenhiemer, once put forward the idea that if a fiction bomb did not work properly it could have other, radically different effects.

"The device works by attacking and rewriting the very fabric of reality. By design, it cuts things out, like editing a movie. But it only works on works of fiction—it can't cut real people out of reality.

"What I think we're seeing here are the effects of a

fiction bomb that backfired. Instead of erasing your work from reality, it made your characters real."

Shatner stood and thought about it for a moment. He looked about the bustling convention floor, his eye stopping to admire a slightly pudgy woman in a two-sizes-too-small Nurse Chapel costume. He turned back to Bob.

"That's…just…stupid."

Bob ignored him and began pacing. "The question is who? Who would want to erase William Shatner?"

He thought hard and then snapped his fingers. "Of course, the Campbellians! They were suspected in the assassination of Adam West last year, but no one could prove anything. I saw one protesting the convention as I came in. I didn't think too much of it at the time."

Bob rushed over to Shatner and grabbed his shoulder. "We've got to get you out of here. We need to get you someplace safe."

"Good God man," said Shatner, "get…a hold of…yourself."

Suddenly a hand grabbed him by the shoulder and spun him around. It was a man holding a walkie-talkie and wearing a "Staff" t-shirt.

"Shit man, where the hell have you been?" asked the man. He raised the walkie-talkie. "Hey, I found Shatner. We're in the Dealer's Room, south side."

"Oh, I've…been about," replied Shatner, "where are the…other guest tables?"

"What other guests?" asked the man.

"I…can't be…the only guest."

"It's called *ShatnerCon,* who else would be invited?"

"I…don't know…any of the hundreds of people I've worked with!"

"Whatever, take it up with Natalie. Not my problem."

Shatner's heart sank. He looked to Bob who was surveying the crowd for any sign of a threat.

I'm the only one here. I'm all alone.

* * *

Kirk ran back and forth from table to table. Stephen slowly walked, barely keeping pace and looking for some method of escape.

Kirk was suddenly right in front of him, leaning in too close.

"How...do...they...know of me," said Kirk with his hands raised in loose fists, "and the history of Starfleet?"

Kirk went to a table and held up a Kirk doll. "They have...toys of me."

He squeezed the doll and it said, "Conquest is easy... control is not."

"Hey man," said the balding dealer from behind the table, "you want to play with that, you've got to pay for that."

Kirk set the doll back down and went to Stephen's side. "This...is a...strange place we find ourselves in...be on guard."

Then Kirk heard a voice that he had never heard before and yet instantly recognized, "I don't know...any of the hundreds of people I've worked with!"

Kirk took out his phaser and raised the weapon. "Be on guard."

Stephen pissed his pants.

* * *

Shatner shook his head and paced back and forth. Bob was trying to convince the staff member of the severity of the situation but he just ignored him and talked on the walkie-talkie.

I'm doomed. Fucked you could even say.

Suddenly, Bob grabbed Shatner and roughly pulled him back. The red beam narrowly missed him and instead hit the staff member, instantly vaporizing him and sending screaming people fleeing for cover.

Shatner and Bob dropped to the ground. Shatner rolled beneath the closest table and crouched up while Bob crawled on all fours to the adjacent row of tables. He slowly raised his head to get a look at his new attacker.

You've got to be shitting me.

Kirk came running around the row of tables and stood where Shatner had just been. He looked around puzzled. Shatner crouched beneath the table and braced both his hands under it. He stood up and heaved, throwing the table and its assortment of Shakespeare plays translated into Klingon at Kirk.

Kirk turned around just in time to not be caught totally off-guard. He braced himself and the table knocked him to his knees.

Shatner turned and quickly scanned the room. Three rows over he saw the glinting steel of a weapon's table.

Bingo.

He threw himself over the first row of tables, knocking over a poster board display of NASA cover-ups.

Shatner came to the next row and the dealer stood defiant on the other side. His hands outstretched and shaking his head, trying to protect his goods. Shatner stopped, surprised. A red beam hit the dealer and he was gone. Shatner dropped to his hands and knees and scurried under the table to get to the weapons.

Kirk confidently walked to where he had lost Shatner. He got to the aisle and saw no sign of him. He crouched down and slowly walked forward, turning around with his phaser raised. He came to the weapon stand that had set up make-shift plastic display walls. Kirk paused and admired a Bushido sword.

Shatner spun around from the corner of the display swinging the curved blade of a Klingon bat'leth. Kirk had just enough time to raise his phaser in defense. The bat'leth knocked the phaser out of his hand, and it went flying high in the air across the room.

Shatner flipped the weapon around and hit Kirk in the gut with the hard wooden handle, sending him falling back. He reached forward and grabbed Kirk's shirt but the flimsy fabric tore away. Kirk landed on his ass, his chest and girdle showing through the ripped uniform.

Seeing this, Stephen was finally shaken out of his terror-induced daze. He saw Kirk fall and he turned and ran.

Kirk saw him. "That's it Redshirt, flank him."

Shatner also picked this time to turn and start running.

Kirk turned and grabbed the nearest object from a table, which happened to be a pewter replica of a Klingon Bird of Prey. Kirk threw it at Shatner, aiming the model for his head.

Shatner ducked just in time and the ship continued to fly.

Stephen turned his head to see if he really was going to escape. The bulbous front of the ship bashed through his right eye and jammed back into his brain, killing him instantly. His corpse toppled over a table and tossed its contents into the air. His head came to rest on a rare hand-written script by Gene Roddenberry. It was an unfilmed episode which featured a much-talked-about Spock/Kirk love scene. The oozing blood from Stephen's head forever ruined the rare work. Some would later argue that this was the greatest loss of the day.

Kirk saw this and from somewhere inside his head a voice said *he's dead Jim*.

Shatner turned to face Kirk and raised the bat'leth. Kirk looked around and grabbed a black tube from another table. A brave fanboy ran up and grabbed the object as well and the two wrestled over it. The fanboy had two feet and a good two hundred pounds on Kirk. Shatner smiled, he was finally getting some help.

The fanboy tossed Kirk about, but Kirk refused to let go of the tube. His thumb found a button on the side. Instantly a red beam shot out into the fanboy's stomach. He let go. Kirk raised the tube and the beam sliced neatly through the fanboy. He fell to his knees as his copious intestines unraveled onto the floor.

Kirk turned around and marveled at the laser-sword as the fanboy tried to put his guts back in

"Oh shit, Captain Kirk's got a lightsaber," someone yelled.

CHAPTER EIGHT

Bruce was getting uneasy about Bruce and Bruce. They were getting too close for the good of the mission. Bruce was having a hard time dealing with all that had been happening and Bruce was too into her and playing the supportive role to see that she was not holding up. Since the Shatners came into the picture, Bruce hadn't stopped crying.

The Shatners.

Bruce didn't like the Shatners. They did not feel right to him. It made him sick to look at them.

There were ten Shatners in their group. Denny Crane seemed to be their leader. Bruce had no idea who Denny Crane was but he claimed to be the greatest lawyer in history. The other Shatners were much less talkative. One, whose clothes and skin were colored like a black and white TV show, seemed to be in a constant state of nervous breakdown. One wore an outfit that reminded Bruce of the outfits at a Renaissance Fair when he was a boy. He walked with his arms limp at his side, his head hung low, and occasionally sighed.

Another of the Shatners danced in front of him and got down on his knees. "This…is…our…destiny."

"Sorry about earlier. You know, with the whole

hitting you thing," said Bruce.

The Shatner ignored him and pranced away.

"What's with him?" muttered Bruce.

"Ignore him," said Crane, "he just wants attention."

* * *

Kirk moved toward Shatner twirling the lightsaber from side to side, the blade instantly devaluing collectibles and severing limbs.

Shatner spun the bat'leth in front of him and stepped forward to meet his combatant.

Kirk swung the lightsaber.

Shatner moved to the side and hit Kirk in the back with the bat'leth's dull side.

Kirk spun around and swiped widely through the air with his weapon.

Shatner dropped to his knees, and the lightsaber went over his head. He attacked again with the bat'leth. This time the sharp side made contact and cut through Kirk's uniform and girdle. The blade slid into his side and black goo splashed out onto Shatner.

Kirk stumbled back and held his wound. He raised the lightsaber and went to make another attack. But before he could, a twelve inch by twelve inch steel Borg ship replica came flying through the air and bounced off the side of his head. Kirk crumbled straight to the floor.

Shatner turned and was horrified to see it was Bob who had saved his life.

Bob rushed forward and grabbed Shatner's arm. "Come on, we got to go."

Shatner looked to the twitching Kirk and did not

really see a better option.

* * *

Kirk lay on the ground flashing in and out of consciousness, his legs jerking uncontrollably. Then he went totally still.

He suddenly sat up. Something did not feel right in his head. He balled his hands into fists and slammed them into his temples, again and again.

He picked up the lightsaber and lurched to his feet. A small crowd of onlookers had now gathered around Kirk. He took two groggy steps forward and then flicked on the lightsaber. When the beam shot out the crowd jumped back.

Kirk smiled and started swinging

There definitely was something wrong with Captain Kirk's head.

CHAPTER NINE

Shatner and Bob raced through the hallways. The convention was now in a total state of mass panic. News of the death and destruction had filtered its way to all the attendees.

"Where...are we going?" asked Shatner as they rushed through another doorway and pushed passed frightened convention goers.

"I don't know," said Bob, "anywhere away from Kirk."

They ran on and then Bob stopped.

"In here," he said as he threw open one of the many nondescript doors that lined the hallway. Shatner ran into the room as Bob looked back to see if Kirk was coming. Luckily for them, he was nowhere in sight. Then Bob ran through the door.

The room was fifty feet wide and went back twenty. The walls were lined with tables loaded down with booze and food and about a dozen metal folding chairs. Gold balloons danced about the ceiling with the air conditioning and the walls draped with gold streams. A few scattered purses and backpacks were about. The partiers must have fled the room in a hurry when everything started going down.

Bob turned the deadbolt on the door and pushed in the knob lock. He leaned against the door and looked around.

"I think we're in the Green Room," he said.

"About...damn time...I...found this place," Shatner said heading for the table piled high with sandwich meat.

"You're braver than I am," said Bob going for the wine and cheese spread, "who knows how long that meat has been sitting out."

"When you've...been on...the convention circuit... as long...as I have," Shatner said through an over-filled mouth, "you...can...handle anything."

Bob snorted and began to gorge himself on fine cheeses. Both men were ravenous. It had been a very eventful day.

Bob heard a very faint sound of movement behind him. It was barely noticeable but he was sure he heard it.

He spun around and heard a much louder noise, like someone ducking for cover. He scanned the room. The room was decently large but there was nowhere for anyone to hide. From where he stood, Bob could see under all the tables. All the chairs were folding chairs, so no one could be hiding behind them. The only door was the door that led back into the hallway and he was sure no one had opened it—the bolt was still locked.

"Hey Bill."

"Yeah," he said through a mashed up combination of salami, brie, and melon balls.

"I think there's someone else in the room."

Shatner froze and forced the mouthful of food down his throat. His head slowly turned as he looked for any sign of an intruder.

"I...don't see...anyone," said Shatner.

"Neither do I," Bob's eyes fiercely narrowed, "but I heard them."

Bob motioned for Shatner to move forward and they began to slowly move across the room. Their senses were on edge, trying to identify the intruder. They made it to the other side of the room, but there was no indication of anybody.

"I think…you're…losing it," said Shatner.

"Wait," said Bob pointing, "that wasn't there before."

In the left corner of the room was a full-sized cardboard cutout of Captain Kirk. The display was not made from a photo-however, it was an artist's rendition of the Starfleet hero done with a sixties pop-art vibe.

"Are you sure…you just…didn't notice it?"

Bob approached the cutout. "Not a chance. This is a display of the woefully short lived *Star Trek: Animated Series* Kirk."

He stood directly in front of Cartoon Kirk and stared intently at the face. "Incredible. I never even knew these were made. I thought I had the full collection of cutouts but somehow I miss—"

Cartoon Kirk blinked.

Bob jumped back and tripped over his own feet. "Holy shit," he gasped as he fell on his ass.

The cutout sprung to life and turned its side to Bob. It was gone.

Bob got to his feet and looked around—there was no sign of Cartoon Kirk.

"You've got to be kidding me," he started walking around the edge of the room in a wide arc. He motioned to Shatner to do the same.

As he passed the cheese table, Bob snatched a large knife off it. Shatner saw this and quickly grabbed his own from a nearby tuna spread.

As they moved around the room a shape began to take form in the center. First it looked like a person sized stick and then, as they moved further around, the shape became the clear form of Cartoon Kirk.

Bob thrust forward the knife. He was getting tired of all this, "Bill, you get him from behind." They began to move at him.

Cartoon Kirk got to his knees and put his face in his hands. "Please...just...do...it."

Shatner and Bob paused in their approach and looked at each other. This was not what they were expecting. They lowered their knives and moved cautiously forward, ready for this to be some kind of trap.

Cartoon Kirk started sobbing, "Please."

They stood around the two-dimensional Shatner. There was no back and front to the living animation. Though Shatner and Bob were on different sides, they looked down at the same sad image of a crying man.

Cartoon Kirk jumped up and spread out his arms wide.

Shatner screamed and jumped back while slashing with the knife. The blade cut through the figure easily, tearing him from the belly-button to just beneath his left armpit—to Bob it was the right.

Everyone froze and stared at the flapping rip. Cartoon Kirk did not lose any sturdiness to his figure and appeared to be otherwise unharmed. He looked down at the cut and dejectedly flopped his arms down. He stared straight ahead at Shatner and Bob.

Bob was getting confused. "Are you...OK?"

"We...do...not...belong here...I...can't...be here," his eyes shifted to meet Shatner and Bob's, "but you...two... do...you are ...real...Shatners."

Bob couldn't help but feel pride well up inside at being called a "real Shatner." THE William Shatner was annoyed.

"But...life is...precious...to live...to be free...why

63

would…anyone want to…give that up?" Shatner asked.

"I…am…a…shadow of a shadow," said Cartoon Kirk weakly, "the others…are angry…I'm not…real enough…for anger…you'd…want…to die too."

They were all silent.

"OK," said Bob, "let's give him what he wants. But how do you propose we do it." He reached forward and batted the cut flap of cartoon flesh with his hand, "this didn't work."

"I…don't…know," said Cartoon Kirk, "but…I…can't live like this."

Shatner thought hard and then snapped his fingers. "Fire."

"Fire?" asked Bob.

"You…ever…see a film reel…burn up…in a projector?"

"Yeah," said Bob, "but where are we going to get fire from."

"The…bags," said Shatner pointing, "the purses… and backpacks…surely one of them…belonged…to a smoker."

Bob nodded and went over to a nearby purse and started digging through it. Shatner found a briefcase and popped it open. Cartoon Kirk watched them without any display of emotion. After checking a few bags, they each found a lighter.

They walked back to Cartoon Kirk

"Are…you…sure about this," asked Shatner.

Cartoon Kirk nodded, "I'm…ready."

Shatner and Bob kneeled down in front of Cartoon Kirk, who crossed his arms over his chest and closed his eyes.

They flicked on the lighters.

"This is the most fucked up thing I've ever done," said Bob.

Simultaneously they put the flames to Cartoon Kirk's feet. Instantly Cartoon Kirk's entire body was engulfed in bright blue flames. Shatner and Bob stepped back as the film stock body began to bubble, crackle, and sizzle. The air smelled like someone was burning tires and cats.

Cartoon Kirk began to lose form and his body started dripping and flowing down to the floor. In under a minute he was reduced to a pile of steaming, bubbling goo.

Shatner and Bob stood over the mess and then walked to the other side of the room where they sat down.

"You still hungry?" asked Bob.

"No."

"Neither am I."

They sat silent. From inside the Green Room all the other sounds of the convention were blocked out. This would be an ideal place to hide. But the smell of burnt Shatner was already getting to Bob and what would they do once the food on the tables ran out or went bad? No, this was no place to live.

"So what should we do?" he asked.

Shatner's brows furrowed as he thought. He looked to the smoldering remains of the Cartoon Kirk. On top of the black sludge a bubble popped.

"We," he looked up at Bob, "have to…get out of here."

CHAPTER TEN

The Shatner sneered as alarmed fans ran around him.

"What? Is someone having a sale on acne cream," he said as people passed by.

He turned around and screamed, "Get a life!"

He continued walking and stopped when he saw the two men who looked exactly like him.

"Good God, look at you," he said to them. The two men spun to face him. Their faces read terror.

"What?" said the Shatner, "are you that surprised to see your idol? The person whose identity you're stealing?"

The Shatner look-alikes looked at each other confused and then back to the Shatner.

"And what the hell happened to you two?" he asked. The two men were wearing identical suits that were torn and dirtied in many places. The one man was covered with bruises and seemed to be bleeding from numerous places.

The two men looked at each other, turned, and continued on their way. The Shatner watched them.

"Losers," he muttered.

* * *

"So there's no way out of here?" asked Bob.

"At least...not through the...doors," replied Shatner as the two of them headed for the stairs.

Shatner had told Bob about the wall of static that was blocking the front entrance. Bob had made it to one of the emergency exits but had found the same barrier. The two had decided to head to the roof and see if the static was surrounding the building.

They entered a room with a large set of stairs in the center that only led up. They walked to the foot of the stairs.

"So what happens if we get to the top and..." Bob went quiet when he looked up the stairs.

Kirk stood at the top brandishing the lightsaber. He was splattered from head to toe in blood. He raised the weapon, roared, and came charging down the stairs.

Shatner and Bob turned and started running back the way they came.

"This has got to stop," yelled Bob as he ran.

Shatner grabbed Bob. "Wait...I have an idea." Shatner turned down a different hallway and Bob followed. Shatner stopped and looked around.

"What, what's your plan?" asked Bob, "hurry up, he's coming."

"OK," Shatner turned to Bob. He spoke as quickly as he could, "Go to the end of the hall and wait for Kirk. I'll hide over there," he gestured to the narrow hallway to their side that led to bathrooms. "Once he's past me, I'll jump him from behind."

Bob looked in the direction of Kirk's oncoming cries.

"Come on," said Shatner, "we have to...do it now."

Shatner quickly dodged into the small hallway and Bob looked at him, worried. Shatner waved his hand motioning for Bob to move back further in the large hallway. Bob slowly moved backwards.

Shatner flattened himself against the wall and waited.

"There you are." Shatner shivered at hearing his own voice.

From his hiding spot, Shatner could see the shadow of Kirk moving down the hall.

Wait. Wait.

The shadow grew larger as Kirk slowly moved. He came into Shatner's vision and took two more steps and stopped. Kirk was now parallel with Shatner and if he just turned his head a little, Shatner would be seen.

Shatner held his breath and tried to will his heart to stop beating so loudly.

Kirk twirled the lightsaber and started moving forward again.

Yes!

Shatner waited a moment and then moved as carefully and quietly as possible to the end of the narrow hall. He peered around the corner. Bob was against the far wall and Kirk had him cornered, the lightsaber poised and ready. Bob saw Shatner and nodded.

Shatner creeped out. He looked at Kirk, then to Bob, and turned and started tip-toeing the other way.

"Hey," called out Bob, "hey!"

Shatner turned back and looked at Bob, his eyes pleading for help. Then he shrugged and inched his way out of the hall.

"You bastard," yelled Bob. He turned to Kirk, "you don't want me. I'm not William Shatner. He's right over there." He pointed at Shatner.

"You must...think...very little of me," Kirk raised the lightsaber high over his head, "for...that...trick to work."

Bob screamed as the lightsaber came down. The blade bisected his body from head to crotch. The two halves fell apart, spilling blood and organs to the floor.

Shatner was at the end of the hall now. As he turned to run, Kirk had turned off the lightsaber and was kneeling down, plunging his hands into the viscera.

* * *

Kirk dug amongst the body. Shatner was now dead, but it didn't feel right. The screaming at the back of his brain—the essential urge that he did not belong in this world—was still there.

He picked up and tossed aside squishy parts of the corpse until he found what he was looking for—the heart. He brought it to his mouth and bit out a huge chunck. He chewed on the tough muscle—fresh blood smeared over his lips and chin—and then spit out the hunk to the floor.

He stood, enraged. He spun around and flipped the lightsaber on.

This was not William Shatner.

CHAPTER ELEVEN

By the time Kirk had realized his mistake, Shatner had made it up two flights of stairs. Without consciously thinking, at the second floor he ran down a hall directly at the top of the stairs. He came to a set of doors and pushed his way through them.

The doors shut behind him and Shatner fell to his hands and knees, exhausted. He wheezed in-and-out. He looked around to find himself in a room about fifty feet by fifty feet. It was lined with tables filled with food and bottles of alcohol. The walls were decorated with streamers and the ceiling was filled with balloons.

Shatner stood up with a groan and stumbled over to the table filled with bottles. He grabbed the whiskey, twisted off the top, and drank deeply from the bottle.

He coughed and leaned against the table.

This is it Bill.

He swigged again from the bottle and stood up straighter. A million tiny cuts and bruises screamed back.

You can't just keep running. He'll just keep coming after you.

He drank more.

You're the hero.

He took a final drink and tossed the bottle across the room.

You're the hero.

He walked over to the room's door.

OK, head to the dealer's room again. The weapons stand should still be well stocked. Either that or find one of those freaky-ass guards. I'll feel safer with them rather than the nerds or psychos.

He opened the door and went through.

I'm the hero—

The briefcase hit him over the head the moment he was through the doorway. Shatner stumbled forward dazed and fell to his knees. He was hit again on the back of his head.

As the world went black he heard a familiar voice yell, "Denny Crane!"

CHAPTER TWELVE

Lobby: People filled all available space and pushed toward the front doors. The wall of static prevented anyone from getting out. Those closest to the doors were crushed and mashed. More and more people surged into the room from all parts of the convention, hoping for some kind of escape. The mass of humanity became denser and denser. Some were sucked beneath the crowd and smashed underfoot.

Dealer's Room: The people had broken down into a tribal mindset and were searching for something, anything, to blame the current disaster on. One target stood out amongst all the others: the Star Wars memorabilia dealers. The crowd rounded them up and herded them into the cleared out center of the room. They circled the dealers and hurled insults.

"Luke is emo."

"George Lucas is the cause of all pain and suffering."

"Han shot second."

The dealers were then pelted with plastic lightsabers and discounted Jar-Jar action figures until they stopped moving.

Theater: Jack and Sondra were convinced this was the end and if they were going down, they were *going down*. They went into theater three and a quick glance made it clear that the room was empty. If Shatner had known how these two people were spending their last minutes, he would have approved.

When they were done, they stood and brushed the gray dust off of each other's bodies. They wondered what the filth was, but they didn't give it too much thought.

Museum: Shatner's senses slowly drifted back. First, he was aware that his legs and arms were restrained and that his head hurt like Hell. His vision came back and he saw he was on a full-scale replica of the bridge of the starship Enterprise—the TV version. He was tied to the Captain's Chair.

Scattered through the bridge were various William Shatners, representing all stages of his career, his life, staring at him. There were also two men and a woman standing together in front of him. Each of them was missing their right hand. Campbellians.

Denny Crane stepped up next to them. "He's awake."

The Campbellians moved and Shatner saw there were two cardboard boxes behind them. One of the men and the woman picked up a box. The other man walked up to Shatner, pulled a package of baby wipes out of his pocket, and began to clean Shatner's head and face.

Shatner shook his head. "What...are...you doing?"

The man punched Shatner in the jaw.

Shatner coughed and spit out a tooth in a mess of blood.

"I only need you to be awake for this," said the Campbellian. He grabbed Shatner's head with one hand and began to wipe it down again with the other. "I don't care what condition you're in."

Shatner stayed still. He looked to the other two

Campbellians. They each had unpacked their boxes. The woman was messing with what looked like an overly large silver VCR. The man held what looked like a large steel motorcycle helmet but it was missing the facemask and it had long wires jutting out of it.

The Campbellian let go of Shatner and the one with the helmet came over and placed it over Shatner's head.

"What...are...you doing to me," asked Shatner.

The Campbellian took hold of the wires from the helmet and plugged them into the back of the VCR-looking device. The woman took a videotape out of the box and put it in the machine.

She pushed a button and then said, "We're good to go."

The first man turned to Shatner. "We're about to steal all your show business knowledge and talent. Everything that has made you a success, we are going to take. It will be a glorious gift for our savior, Bruce."

All three Campbellians raised their handless right arms and lowered their heads. They were silent for a moment and then they lowered their arms.

The man continued, "What I need you to do is think about your life. To help you along, when I'm done, they're," the Campbellian motioned with his head to the Shatners, "going to kill you."

"Wait...I...implore you," said Shatner, "you...don't have to do this...are we not all...humans...people...people with hopes...dreams...and desires...think for yourself... your God...is a lie...do the right thing...let me...go."

"Nope," the man moved away from Shatner and turned to the woman who was crouched in front of the other machine.

"Do it," he said.

Before she had a chance to push the button, Denny Crane jumped in between them.

"Wait," he yelled.

"Why?" asked the Campbellian who was standing off to the side.

Crane turned to him and smiled, "for suspense."

"Fuck him," said the other male Campbellian. He turned to the woman, "Push-"

Before he could finish, the tuborlift beeped. Everyone in the room turned to it as the doors slid open. A blood-slicked, crazed-eyed Captain Kirk stepped out.

The room was frozen in shock as Kirk slowly turned his head, eyeing them all. He held out his right hand, which held the lightsaber, and flicked the weapon on. The room was still and silent as everyone waited to see who would make the first move.

The tuborlift on the other side of the room beeped and its doors slid open. Out stepped another Shatner.

"Welcome back to this special convention edition of 'Rescue 911,'" he said staring off, "here, on the bridge of the Enterprise, was the site of one of the convention's bloodiest and most bizarre incidents. As a deranged Captain Kirk brutally massacred a room full of terrorists and fictional characters made real."

Kirk roared and charged the nearest Shatner, who looked circa mid-seventies, and drop-kicked him.

The Shatners rushed to Kirk.

"You...people...are crazy," yelled William Shatner from beneath the helmet.

Kirk leapt to his feet and swung the lightsaber at the Shatner dressed in old-English garb that was running towards him. The beam smoothly decapitated him and sent his head rolling across the bridge.

The black-and-white Shatner tried attacking Kirk from behind but he spun around and quickly struck with the weapon, neatly cutting off both of his arms. The stumps sprayed black sludge and film stock as the Shatner slumped to the floor.

"Remember, everything you're seeing is real," said Rescue 911 Shatner, still standing at the second tuborlift.

The Campbellians watched as Kirk began the slaughter. Blood and limbs flew about the room.

The Campbellian closest to Shatner turned to face the others, "Start the machine."

The woman pushed a button on the machine and Shatner started convulsing in the captain's chair. He screamed as the machine began to steal his identity. It felt like a thousand straws had been stuck in his skull and the insides were being slowly sucked out. His consciousness flickered out and Shatner found himself only aware of his memories as they were dismantled piece by piece. He was lost in his own internal, crumbling world.

The Campbellian closest to Shatner shook his fists in the air. "Yes. Yes! All glory be to Bru—"

He stopped and looked down. A bright beam of red light jutted from his chest. It sunk back into to his chest and the Campbellian fell to the ground.

Kirk stepped over the corpse and charged the other Campbellians, widely waving the lightsaber. The man jumped aside. The woman screamed and dodged, falling over the recording device, as the glowing blade narrowly missing her

Blood began to flow from William Shatner's nose and the corners of his eyes. Green, creamy pus slowly oozed out of his ears. He pissed and shit himself at the same time. Having who you are sucked out of your head is an extremely unpleasant experience.

Kirk stood over the woman and brought the light-saber down. She rolled to the side and the machine beneath her was cut in half.

Shatner began screaming as the helmet, with now no destination to send the information it was collecting, began sending the data feedback into his skull. Every millisecond that passed, Shatner's memory doubled, but it was all the same info. After a moment, Shatner had a thousand memories of his first kiss. His head felt on the verge of explosion as more and more info was crammed into it.

Kirk turned his attention to the screaming and walked over to William Shatner. He raised the lightsaber to his left side. Shatner kept screaming, unaware of anything but his past as it filled and refilled his head.

Kirk swung and cut Shatner's head in half, long-ways. The room went silent as every eye watched the half skull flip through the air, flinging brain matter. It hit the floor with a *CLUNK.*

A bright beam of white light shot up from the attached half of Shatner's head. It looked like someone had turned on a spotlight in the body.

Bruce and Bruce ran to each other and clutched tight.

As one, all the Shatners dropped to their knees and raised their fists.

"NNNNNOOOOO," they all screamed.

Their hands began to lose form. Their finger fused together and stretched out with a sickening cracking sound. The tissue pulled and reshaped into a series of bone squares framing translucent skin. The flesh film-strips stretched through in the air and went into Shatner's skull and the source of the light.

The Shatners screamed as their bodies bent and transformed. First their arms were gone. Then the Shatners levitated into the air as their feet began to change. Their legs disappeared as the limbs fused together and extended out, giving each body a third reel. Once the makeover completely took their arms, their torsos began to change starting at the shoulder. The three reels of flesh-stock met in the center of the chest and became one large strip continuing up to their neck.

The floating disembodied Shatner heads managed to sustain the cry of "No!" until they too disappeared.

The flesh-strips flapped in the air and then were sucked into the light. Once the last bit was gone, the light suddenly turned off.

Bruce and Bruce stood silent and still. They looked at each other and then to Shatner's body. Blood oozed down the half-head.

They turned to each other. Bruce stared deeply into Bruce's eyes.

"I think it's all over," Bruce said.

Bruce nodded. "There's something I've wanted to tell you," she said.

"Yes," said Bruce.

"I love—"

The blast of red light emitted from Shatner's head. It tore through the room, leaving all non-living matter unharmed but it reduced Bruce and Bruce's brains to runny sludge as it passed through them. They fell to the ground holding each other.

The light spread through the whole convention center. It filled every room and overtook everyone.

Then the light went out.

CHAPTER THIRTEEN

William Shatner came to. He moved his head and it felt like a thousand Gorn were pounding inside. He winced at the pain as he looked around the room. It was empty but for the three Campbellians lying on the ground. One had a gaping hole through his chest. The other two didn't look harmed but they were not breathing.

He tried moving his body and the rope that had held his arms and legs in place easily broke away. He looked at it and it looked like it had been burned through.

He turned around in the chair and looked behind him. There really was no one else in the room.

Where did the...me's go?

The last thing he could remember was the Campbellians putting the helmet on his head. Then he went out.

He looked down at his body and saw that his clothes were now fresh and clean. It was the same suit he had been wearing before but all the blood stains and tears were gone, as if he had not been fighting for his life all day.

As he tried to stand up, the world violently spun about him. He tried to steady himself but he fell right back into the captain's chair.

He tried standing again and he fell to the floor. Struggling, he managed to get to his hands and knees. His head screamed in protest at the movement.

The turned-off lightsaber was on the floor in front of him. He grabbed it and shoved it in the waistband of his pants. If any of the Shatners were around, they would surely make short work of him in this condition but at least the weapon would give him a fighting chance.

He crawled to the door of the tuborlift and pulled himself up the wall. He paused to vomit and then the world had stopped moving slightly enough for him to stand on his own. He pushed the button and the doors slid open.

The next room of the museum, an exhibit based on "Incubus," was empty of people. So was the next one. Shatner did not see any sign of another person until he managed to stagger to the lobby.

The marble floors were carpeted with corpses. Some had obviously been crushed to death by the crowd, their bodies mangled and mashed. Some bodies displayed no signs of injury but it was obvious from their positions and stillness that they were all dead.

Shatner stood at the top of the lobby's stairs and almost cried when he saw the sun shining in through the glass entranceway. He half ran/half fell down the stairs and across the bodies. His head and body screamed with pain in protest but he was too joyous to care.

He reached the set of doors next to the wrecked ambulance and with great effort, managed to push aside the body of a skinny girl wearing Spock ears.

He went into the revolving doors and pushed and found himself outside. He rushed forward and threw himself onto the concrete. The feel of fresh air as euphoric as a drug to him.

He was vaguely aware of the flashing lights of emergency vehicles around him and only half-heard the person run up to him.

"Are you OK, sir?" they asked, throwing a blanket over him.

Shatner didn't respond. He just cried and started kissing the ground.

The person pulled him to his feet as two other people ran over. They guided him to the back of an ambulance as they talked. Shatner's head hung low the whole time. The pain had receeded but there was now a low drone that filled his hearing.

"Is it…"

"I think so."

"Sir? Sir? Are you OK? Can you tell me your name?"

Shatner slumped against the side of the ambulance and started laughing, "I'm…William Shatner."

He laughed so hard his eyes teared up. He rolled his head around giggling.

When he looked at the paramedics he started screaming.

CHAPTER FOURTEEN

The bar was darkly lit and people disappeared into shadows along the wall. It was just what Shatner was looking for. He found a stool at the bar and took a seat. His head ached with a dull throb.

The bartender came over. "What can I get you?"

William Shatner looked into his own face. "Whiskey…on the rocks."

The bartender placed down the drink and Shatner paid, tipping generously.

He reached into his pocket and pulled out a bottle of pills. He popped three in his mouth and downed them with a swallow of whiskey. The bartender watched this happen but said nothing and left to attend to other customers.

Shatner sipped his drink and looked around the room. He saw himself sitting at three other spots at the bar, a group of four hims were at a table, and two of him were making out in a back corner booth.

He chugged the rest of the drink, his head feeling slightly better as the drug cocktail numbed him, and waved the bartender over for another. He spent the rest of the night with his head low, slamming back whiskey and downing pills.

The bartender announced last call and Shatner stood

up, preparing to leave.

"Excuse me, are you William Shatner?"

He turned and saw himself wearing a very short, very tight red dress.

The Shatner batted his eyes at him and held out his hand. "It's an honor to meet you. I've been a fan for a long time. A *very* long time."

Shatner looked at the hand. "Thanks." He turned and headed for the exit.

The Shatner jumped in front of him. "This may be a bit forward of me, but, my place is just around the corner. Would you care to come over for a...nightcap?"

Shatner looked at himself. Somewhere in the back of his brain was that constant pain but the one-two punch of alcohol and painkillers was taking care of that for now. *What the Hell.* He had to admit, he was a fine-looking man.

The two went out the bar's doors together. The Shatner put his (her?) arm around him and guided him away from the bar.

"Give me some sugar baby," yelled someone from across the street.

Shatner turned around and saw a Shatner wearing a long black coat on the other side of the street. The Shatner threw open the coat and two things were apparent:

1: He was missing his right hand.

2: He was wearing a vest of dynamite.

The Shatner began running across the street towards him. Shatner let go of his hook-up and ran to meet him.

They met in the middle of the road. William Shatner wrapped one arm tightly around the Campbellian's waist and the other around his neck, and then dipped him low. The Shatner looked up in shock as Shatner stared deeply into his eyes. He kissed him as the bomb went off.

To Jeff,
Love the Book
William Shatner

ABOUT THE AUTHOR

Jeff Burk lives in Portland, OR where he edits *The Magazine of Bizarro Fiction.* He spends much of his time avoiding copyright lawsuits and organizing cat militias. He has never met William Shatner—yet.

CATALOG   SPRING 2010

Bizarro Books publishes under the following imprints:

www.rawdogscreamingpress.com

www.eraserheadpress.com

www.afterbirthbooks.com

www.swallowdownpress.com

For all your Bizarro needs visit:

WWW.BIZARROCENTRAL.COM

Introduce yourselves to the bizarro genre and all of its authors with the Bizarro Starter Kit series. Each volume features short novels and short stories by ten of the leading bizarro authors, designed to give you a perfect sampling of the genre for only $5 plus shipping.

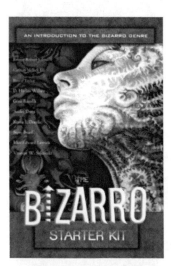

BB-0X1
"The Bizarro Starter Kit"
(Orange)

Featuring D. Harlan Wilson, Carlton Mellick III, Jeremy Robert Johnson, Kevin L Donihe, Gina Ranalli, Andre Duza, Vincent W. Sakowski, Steve Beard, John Edward Lawson, and Bruce Taylor.

236 pages $5

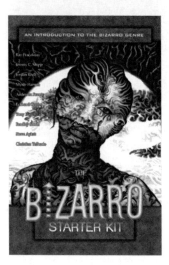

BB-0X2
"The Bizarro Starter Kit"
(Blue)

Featuring Ray Fracalossy, Jeremy C. Shipp, Jordan Krall, Mykle Hansen, Andersen Prunty, Eckhard Gerdes, Bradley Sands, Steve Aylett, Christian TeBordo, and Tony Rauch.

244 pages $5

BB-001 "The Kafka Effekt" D. Harlan Wilson - A collection of forty-four irreal short stories loosely written in the vein of Franz Kafka, with more than a pinch of William S. Burroughs sprinkled on top. **211 pages $14**

BB-002 "Satan Burger" Carlton Mellick III - The cult novel that put Carlton Mellick III on the map ... Six punks get jobs at a fast food restaurant owned by the devil in a city violently overpopulated by surreal alien cultures. **236 pages $14**

BB-003 "Some Things Are Better Left Unplugged" Vincent Sakwoski - Join The Man and his Nemesis, the obese tabby, for a nightmare roller coaster ride into this postmodern fantasy. **152 pages $10**

BB-004 "Shall We Gather At the Garden?" Kevin L Donihe - Donihe's Debut novel. Midgets take over the world, The Church of Lionel Richie vs. The Church of the Byrds, plant porn and more! **244 pages $14**

BB-005 "Razor Wire Pubic Hair" Carlton Mellick III - A genderless humandildo is purchased by a razor dominatrix and brought into her nightmarish world of bizarre sex and mutilation. **176 pages $11**

BB-006 "Stranger on the Loose" D. Harlan Wilson - The fiction of Wilson's 2nd collection is planted in the soil of normalcy, but what grows out of that soil is a dark, witty, otherworldly jungle... **228 pages $14**

BB-007 "The Baby Jesus Butt Plug" Carlton Mellick III - Using clones of the Baby Jesus for anal sex will be the hip sex fetish of the future. **92 pages $10**

BB-008 "Fishyfleshed" Carlton Mellick III - The world of the past is an illogical flatland lacking in dimension and color, a sick-scape of crispy squid people wandering the desert for no apparent reason. **260 pages $14**

BB-009 **"Dead Bitch Army" Andre Duza** - Step into a world filled with racist teenagers, cannibals, 100 warped Uncle Sams, automobiles with razor-sharp teeth, living graffiti, and a pissed-off zombie bitch out for revenge. **344 pages $16**

BB-010 **"The Menstruating Mall" Carlton Mellick III** - "The Breakfast Club meets Chopping Mall as directed by David Lynch." - Brian Keene **212 pages $12**

BB-011 **"Angel Dust Apocalypse" Jeremy Robert Johnson** - Meth-heads, man-made monsters, and murderous Neo-Nazis. "Seriously amazing short stories..." - Chuck Palahniuk, author of Fight Club **184 pages $11**

BB-012 **"Ocean of Lard" Kevin L Donihe / Carlton Mellick III** - A parody of those old Choose Your Own Adventure kid's books about some very odd pirates sailing on a sea made of animal fat. **176 pages $12**

BB-013 **"Last Burn in Hell" John Edward Lawson** - From his lurid angst-affair with a lesbian music diva to his ascendance as unlikely pop icon the one constant for Kenrick Brimley, official state prison gigolo, is he's got no clue what he's doing. **172 pages $14**

BB-014 **"Tangerinephant" Kevin Dole 2** - TV-obsessed aliens have abducted Michael Tangerinephant in this bizarro combination of science fiction, satire, and surrealism. **164 pages $11**

BB-015 **"Foop!" Chris Genoa** - Strange happenings are going on at Dactyl, Inc, the world's first and only time travel tourism company.

"A surreal pie in the face!" - Christopher Moore **300 pages $14**

BB-016 **"Spider Pie" Alyssa Sturgill** - A one-way trip down a rabbit hole inhabited by sexual deviants and friendly monsters, fairytale beginnings and hideous endings. **104 pages $11**

BB-017 "The Unauthorized Woman" Efrem Emerson - Enter the world of the inner freak, a landscape populated by the pre-dead and morticioners, by cockroaches and 300-lb robots. **104 pages $11**

BB-018 "Fugue XXIX" Forrest Aguirre - Tales from the fringe of speculative literary fiction where innovative minds dream up the future's uncharted territories while mining forgotten treasures of the past. **220 pages $16**

BB-019 "Pocket Full of Loose Razorblades" John Edward Lawson - A collection of dark bizarro stories. From a giant rectum to a foot-fungus factory to a girl with a biforked tongue. **190 pages $13**

BB-020 "Punk Land" Carlton Mellick III - In the punk version of Heaven, the anarchist utopia is threatened by corporate fascism and only Goblin, Mortician's sperm, and a blue-mohawked female assassin named Shark Girl can stop them. **284 pages $15**

BB-021 "Pseudo-City" D. Harlan Wilson - Pseudo-City exposes what waits in the bathroom stall, under the manhole cover and in the corporate boardroom, all in a way that can only be described as mind-bogglingly irreal. **220 pages $16**

BB-022 "Kafka's Uncle and Other Strange Tales" Bruce Taylor - Anslenot and his giant tarantula (tormentor? fri-end?) wander a desecrated world in this novel and collection of stories from Mr. Magic Realism Himself. **348 pages $17**

BB-023 "Sex and Death In Television Town" Carlton Mellick III - In the old west, a gang of hermaphrodite gunslingers take refuge from a demon plague in Telos: a town where its citizens have televisions instead of heads. **184 pages $12**

BB-024 "It Came From Below The Belt" Bradley Sands - What can Grover Goldstein do when his severed, sentient penis forces him to return to high school and help it win the presidential election? **204 pages $13**

BB-025 "Sick: An Anthology of Illness" John Lawson, editor - These Sick stories are horrendous and hilarious dissections of creative minds on the scalpel's edge. **296 pages $16**

BB-026 "Tempting Disaster" John Lawson, editor - A shocking and alluring anthology from the fringe that examines our culture's obsession with taboos. **260 pages $16**

BB-027 "Siren Promised" Jeremy Robert Johnson - Nominated for the Bram Stoker Award. A potent mix of bad drugs, bad dreams, brutal bad guys, and surreal/incredible art by Alan M. Clark. **190 pages $13**

BB-028 "Chemical Gardens" Gina Ranalli - Ro and punk band Green is the Enemy find Kreepkins, a surfer-dude warlock, a vengeful demon, and a Metal Priestess in their way as they try to escape an underground nightmare. **188 pages $13**

BB-029 "Jesus Freaks" Andre Duza - For God so loved the world that he gave his only two begotten sons… and a few million zombies. **400 pages $16**

BB-030 "Grape City" Kevin L. Donihe - More Donihe-style comedic bizarro about a demon named Charles who is forced to work a minimum wage job on Earth after Hell goes out of business. **108 pages $10**

BB-031"Sea of the Patchwork Cats" Carlton Mellick III - A quiet dreamlike tale set in the ashes of the human race. For Mellick enthusiasts who also adore The Twilight Zone. **112 pages $10**

BB-032 "Extinction Journals" Jeremy Robert Johnson - An uncanny voyage across a newly nuclear America where one man must confront the problems associated with loneliness, insane dieties, radiation, love, and an ever-evolving cockroach suit with a mind of its own. **104 pages $10**

BB-033 **"Meat Puppet Cabaret" Steve Beard** - At last! The secret connection between Jack the Ripper and Princess Diana's death revealed! **240 pages $16 / $30**

BB-034 **"The Greatest Fucking Moment in Sports" Kevin L. Donihe** - In the tradition of the surreal anti-sitcom Get A Life comes a tale of triumph and agape love from the master of comedic bizarro. **108 pages $10**

BB-035 **"The Troublesome Amputee" John Edward Lawson** - Disturbing verse from a man who truly believes nothing is sacred and intends to prove it. **104 pages $9**

BB-036 **"Deity" Vic Mudd** - God (who doesn't like to be called "God") comes down to a typical, suburban, Ohio family for a little vacation—but it doesn't turn out to be as relaxing as He had hoped it would be... **168 pages $12**

BB-037 **"The Haunted Vagina" Carlton Mellick III** - It's difficult to love a woman whose vagina is a gateway to the world of the dead. **132 pages $10**

BB-038 **"Tales from the Vinegar Wasteland" Ray Fracalossy** - Witness: a man is slowly losing his face, a neighbor who periodically screams out for no apparent reason, and a house with a room that doesn't actually exist. **240 pages $14**

BB-039 **"Suicide Girls in the Afterlife" Gina Ranalli** - After Pogue commits suicide, she unexpectedly finds herself an unwilling "guest" at a hotel in the Afterlife, where she meets a group of bizarre characters, including a goth Satan, a hippie Jesus, and an alien-human hybrid. **100 pages $9**

BB-040 **"And Your Point Is?" Steve Aylett** - In this follow-up to LINT multiple authors provide critical commentary and essays about Jeff Lint's mind-bending literature. **104 pages $11**

BB-041 **"Not Quite One of the Boys" Vincent Sakowski** - While drug-dealer Maxi drinks with Dante in purgatory, God and Satan play a little tri-level chess and do a little bargaining over his business partner, Vinnie, who is still left on earth. **220 pages $14**

BB-042 **"Teeth and Tongue Landscape" Carlton Mellick III** - On a planet made out of meat, a socially-obsessive monophobic man tries to find his place amongst the strange creatures and communities that he comes across. **110 pages $10**

BB-043 **"War Slut" Carlton Mellick III** - Part "1984," part "Waiting for Godot," and part action horror video game adaptation of John Carpenter's "The Thing." **116 pages $10**

BB-044 **"All Encompassing Trip" Nicole Del Sesto** - In a world where coffee is no longer available, the only television shows are reality TV re-runs, and the animals are talking back, Nikki, Amber and a singing Coyote in a do-rag are out to restore the light **308 pages $15**

BB-045 **"Dr. Identity" D. Harlan Wilson** - Follow the Dystopian Duo on a killing spree of epic proportions through the irreal postcapitalist city of Bliptown where time ticks sideways, artificial Bug-Eyed Monsters punish citizens for consumer-capitalist lethargy, and ultraviolence is as essential as a daily multivitamin. **208 pages $15**

BB-046 **"The Million-Year Centipede" Eckhard Gerdes** - Wakelin, frontman for 'The Hinge,' wrote a poem so prophetic that to ignore it dooms a person to drown in blood. **130 pages $12**

BB-047 **"Sausagey Santa" Carlton Mellick III** - A bizarro Christmas tale featuring Santa as a piratey mutant with a body made of sausages. 124 pages $10

BB-048 **"Misadventures in a Thumbnail Universe" Vincent Sakowski** - Dive deep into the surreal and satirical realms of neo-classical Blender Fiction, filled with television shoes and flesh-filled skies. **120 pages $10**

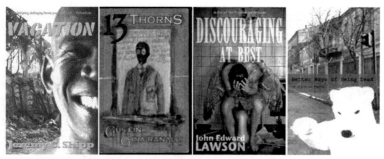

BB-049 **"Vacation" Jeremy C. Shipp** - Blueblood Bernard Johnson leaved his boring life behind to go on The Vacation, a year-long corporate sponsored odyssey. But instead of seeing the world, Bernard is captured by terrorists, becomes a key figure in secret drug wars, and, worse, doesn't once miss his secure American Dream. **160 pages $14**

BB-051 **"13 Thorns" Gina Ranalli** - Thirteen tales of twisted, bizarro horror. **240 pages $13**

BB-050 **"Discouraging at Best" John Edward Lawson** - A collection where the absurdity of the mundane expands exponentially creating a tidal wave that sweeps reason away. For those who enjoy satire, bizarro, or a good old-fashioned slap to the senses. **208 pages $15**

BB-052 **"Better Ways of Being Dead" Christian TeBordo** - In this class, the students have to keep one palm down on the table at all times, and listen to lectures about a panda who speaks Chinese. **216 pages $14**

BB-053 **"Ballad of a Slow Poisoner" Andrew Goldfarb** Millford Mutterwurst sat down on a Tuesday to take his afternoon tea, and made the unpleasant discovery that his elbows were becoming flatter. **128 pages $10**

BB-054 **"Wall of Kiss" Gina Ranalli** - A woman... A wall... Sometimes love blooms in the strangest of places. **108 pages $9**

BB-055 **"HELP! A Bear is Eating Me" Mykle Hansen** - The bizarro, heartwarming, magical tale of poor planning, hubris and severe blood loss... **150 pages $11**

BB-056 **"Piecemeal June" Jordan Krall** - A man falls in love with a living sex doll, but with love comes danger when her creator comes after her with crab-squid assassins. **90 pages $9**

BB-057 **"Laredo" Tony Rauch** - Dreamlike, surreal stories by Tony Rauch. **180 pages $12**

BB-058 **"The Overwhelming Urge" Andersen Prunty** - A collection of bizarro tales by Andersen Prunty. **150 pages $11**

BB-059 **"Adolf in Wonderland" Carlton Mellick III** - A dreamlike adventure that takes a young descendant of Adolf Hitler's design and sends him down the rabbit hole into a world of imperfection and disorder. **180 pages $11**

BB-060 **"Super Cell Anemia" Duncan B. Barlow** - "Unrelentingly bizarre and mysterious, unsettling in all the right ways..." - Brian Evenson. **180 pages $12**

BB-061 **"Ultra Fuckers" Carlton Mellick III** - Absurdist suburban horror about a couple who enter an upper middle class gated community but can't find their way out. **108 pages $9**

BB-062 **"House of Houses" Kevin L. Donihe** - An odd man wants to marry his house. Unfortunately, all of the houses in the world collapse at the same time in the Great House Holocaust. Now he must travel to House Heaven to find his departed fiancee. **172 pages $11**

BB-063 **"Necro Sex Machine" Andre Duza** - The Dead Bitch returns in this follow-up to the bizarro zombie epic Dead Bitch Army. **400 pages $16**

BB-064 **"Squid Pulp Blues" Jordan Krall** - In these three bizarro-noir novellas, the reader is thrown into a world of murderers, drugs made from squid parts, deformed gun-toting veterans, and a mischievous apocalyptic donkey. **204 pages $12**

BB-065 **"Jack and Mr. Grin" Andersen Prunty** - "When Mr. Grin calls you can hear a smile in his voice. Not a warm and friendly smile, but the kind that seizes your spine in fear. You don't need to pay your phone bill to hear it. That smile is in every line of Prunty's prose." - Tom Bradley. **208 pages $12**

BB-066 **"Cybernetrix" Carlton Mellick III** - What would you do if your normal everyday world was slowly mutating into the video game world from Tron? **212 pages $12**

BB-067 **"Lemur" Tom Bradley** - Spencer Sproul is a would-be serial-killing bus boy who can't manage to murder, injure, or even scare anybody. However, there are other ways to do damage to far more people and do it legally... **120 pages $12**

BB-068 **"Cocoon of Terror" Jason Earls** - Decapitated corpses...a sculpture of terror...Zelian's masterpiece, his Cocoon of Terror, will trigger a supernatural disaster for everyone on Earth. **196 pages $14**

BB-069 **"Mother Puncher" Gina Ranalli** - The world has become tragically over-populated and now the government strongly opposes procreation. Ed is employed by the government as a mother-puncher. He doesn't relish his job, but he knows it has to be done and he knows he's the best one to do it. **120 pages $9**

BB-070 **"My Landlady the Lobotomist" Eckhard Gerdes** - The brains of past tenants line the shelves of my boarding house, soaking in a mysterious elixir. One more slip-up and the landlady might just add my frontal lobe to her collection. **116 pages $12**

BB-071 **"CPR for Dummies" Mickey Z.** - This hilarious freakshow at the world's end is the fragmented, sobering debut novel by acclaimed nonfiction author Mickey Z. **216 pages $14**

BB-072 **"Zerostrata" Andersen Prunty** - Hansel Nothing lives in a tree house, suffers from memory loss, has a very eccentric family, and falls in love with a woman who runs naked through the woods every night. **144 pages $11**

BB-073 "The Egg Man" Carlton Mellick III - It is a world where humans reproduce like insects. Children are the property of corporations, and having an enormous ten-foot brain implanted into your skull is a grotesque sexual fetish. Mellick's industrial urban dystopia is one of his darkest and grittiest to date. **184 pages $11**

BB-074 "Shark Hunting in Paradise Garden" Cameron Pierce - A group of strange humanoid religious fanatics travel back in time to the Garden of Eden to discover it is invested with hundreds of giant flying maneating sharks. **150 pages $10**

BB-075 "Apeshit" Carlton Mellick III - Friday the 13th meets Visitor Q. Six hipster teens go to a cabin in the woods inhabited by a deformed killer. An incredibly fucked-up parody of B-horror movies with a bizarro slant. **192 pages $12**

BB-076 "Fuckers of Everything on the Crazy Shitting Planet of the Vomit At smosphere" Mykle Hansen - Three bizarro satires. Monster Cocks, Journey to the Center of Agnes Cuddlebottom, and Crazy Shitting Planet. **228 pages $12**

BB-077 "The Kissing Bug" Daniel Scott Buck - In the tradition of Roald Dahl, Tim Burton, and Edward Gorey, comes this bizarro anti-war children's story about a bohemian conenose kissing bug who falls in love with a human woman. **116 pages $10**

BB-078 "MachoPoni" Lotus Rose - It's My Little Pony... *Bizarro* style! A long time ago Poniworld was split in two. On one side of the Jagged Line is the Pastel Kingdom, a magical land of music, parties, and positivity. On the other side of the Jagged Line is Dark Kingdom inhabited by an army of undead ponies. **148 pages $11**

BB-079 "The Faggiest Vampire" Carlton Mellick III - A Roald Dahl-esque children's story about two faggy vampires who partake in a mustache competition to find out which one is truly the faggiest. **104 pages $10**

BB-080 "Sky Tongues" Gina Ranalli - The autobiography of Sky Tongues, the biracial hermaphrodite actress with tongues for fingers. Follow her strange life story as she rises from freak to fame. **204 pages $12**

COMING SOON

"Washer Mouth" by Kevin L. Donihe
"The Cannibals of Candy Land" by Carlton Mellick III
"Fistful of Feet" by Jordan Krall
"Ass Goblins of Auschwitz" by Cameron Pierce
"Cursed" by Jeremy C. Shipp

ORDER FORM

TITLES	QTY	PRICE	TOTAL

Please make checks and moneyorders payable to ROSE O'KEEFE / BIZARRO BOOKS in U.S. funds only. Please don't send bad checks! Allow 2-6 weeks for delivery. International orders may take longer. If you'd like to pay online via PAYPAL.COM, send payments to publisher@eraserheadpress.com.

SHIPPING: US ORDERS - $2 for the first book, $1 for each additional book. For priority shipping, add an additional $4. INT'L ORDERS - $5 for the first book, $3 for each additional book. Add an additional $5 per book for global priority shipping.

Send payment to:

BIZARRO BOOKS
C/O Rose O'Keefe
205 NE Bryant
Portland, OR 97211

Address		
City	State	Zip
Email	Phone	

Lightning Source UK Ltd.
Milton Keynes UK
UKOW03f1829221013

219576UK00010B/210/P